MURDER

The Truth about Gossip

Thanks Shelma

MARQUI ANTWON W. TAYLOR

Palmetto Publishing Group
Charleston, SC

Murder
Copyright © 2018 by Marqui Antwon W. Taylor

All rights reserved
No portion of this book may be reproduced, stored in a retrieval system, or transmitted in any form by any means—electronic, mechanical, photocopy, recording, or other—except for brief quotations in printed reviews, without prior permission of the author.

First Edition

Printed in the United States

ISBN-13: 978-1-64111-288-8
ISBN-10: 1-64111-288-3

TABLE OF CONTENTS

Dedication		v
Acknowledgements		vii
Introduction		ix
Chapter 1	Origin	1
Chapter 2	A Diabolic Plan	5
Chapter 3	More Than Words	12
Chapter 4	But It's True	20
Chapter 5	The Grapevine	26
Chapter 6	Judgment	30
Chapter 7	Deliverance	34

DEDICATION

This book is dedicated to the memories of Betty Lee Cannon and Blondell T. Taylor. I'm still trying to sing like the both of you.

ACKNOWLEDGEMENTS

When I call to remembrance the unfeigned faith that is in thee, which dwelt first in thy grandmother Lois, and thy mother Eunice; and I am persuaded that is in thee also.
—2 Timothy 1:5

This is absolutely my favorite verse of scripture because Paul could not have been more accurate if he had been writing this to me. I am who I am in God because of my grandmother, Frances L. Williamson, and my mother, Tamekia Williamson-Taylor.

Thanks, Grandmamma, for my earliest memory of the power of prayer. I'll never forget that Saturday morning as a little boy when we were dragged with you to visit the sick and shut-in. Before leaving one house in particular, you prayed, and the tangible presence of God filled the room. The feeling I experienced that day keeps me running back to the throne today.

Thanks, Tamekia, for influencing me in the areas of public speaking, writing, the arts, and the study of the Word through your example.

Finally, to Malachi Taylor, you are God's man for your generation. Poppa's expecting great things from you.

INTRODUCTION

In seminary, I was an accessory after the fact. I—a twenty-one-year-old, very impressionable undergrad young preacher—was invited into the company of three accomplished graduate-level ministers for breakfast. These had influence in the city and could get me in the right circles to really propel my ministry. So, in anticipation of a morning of typical doctrine talk, bragging, and stories, I prepared by recollecting my best hermeneutical revelations with which to impress the guys.

As the afternoon drew on in the company of the preachers, I became more impressed to know that some of their reaches were broader than I had initially expected. They were friends with world-famous ministry personalities. And I'm not talking Facebook friends. They were really personal, cell-phone-contact friends with these people.

Then the daggers began flying, totally assassinating these folks' characters. I left the breakfast table that morning with blood splatter all over me.

Being a church boy in every traditional sense of the word, gossip was no big deal to me until I experienced its crushing blow myself. I, like most other Christians, had a doctrinal concurrence that gossiping was wrong, but I still engaged in it. I call this a domestic dichotomy; Paul outlines it in Romans 7:15–25. The apostle's inward struggle was not unlike mine; he said, "I know right from wrong, but when it comes down to it, I end up doing the very thing I hate." Hear the frustration in Paul's voice as he exclaims: "O wretched man that I am! Who shall deliver from the body of this death?"

In this book we will delve into the truth about gossip, how one can be delivered from its constricting grip, and what the enemy is cunningly doing to Christianity with what others have termed an "innocent infraction." Gossip is not just an infraction. Let's begin this book by calling it what it is: sin.

CHAPTER 1

ORIGIN

12 How art thou fallen from heaven, O Lucifer, son of the morning! how art thou cut down to the ground, which didst weaken the nations! 13 For thou hast said in thine heart, I will ascend in to heaven, I will exalt my throne above the stars of God: I will sit also upon the mount of the congregation, in the side of the north:14 I will ascend above the heights of the clouds; I will be like the most High.
—Isaiah 14:12–14

In verse 12, we learn that Satan's name was once Lucifer. He was of a class of angels called seraphim. Lucifer was privileged to lead the angels in the worship of God, but this wasn't enough for him. Notice that both statements in verse 12 are punctuated with exclamation points, as if to beg, "How asinine must one be to relinquish such a position of honor?" But this pride would prove to be Satan's undoing, and the book of Revelation records the whole debacle: "And his tail drew the third part of the stars of heaven, and did cast them to the earth" (Rev.12:4). "7 And there was war in heaven: Michael and his angels fought against the dragon; and the dragon fought and his angels, 8 And prevailed not; neither was there place found any more in heaven. 9 And the great dragon was cast out, that old serpent, called the Devil, and Satan, which deceiveth the whole world: he was cast out into the earth: and his angels were cast out with him." (Rev.12:7–9).

Revelation 12:4 teaches us that a third of the angels fell along with Satan. Notice that the scripture says they were drawn (or lured) by Satan, which denotes that these angels were not predestined to fall but willfully submitted to Satan. So, away with this notion that angels have no will.

But how were these particular angels ever persuaded to leave the protection of their creator to follow a renegade? The answer is gossip. Satan used the influence that God had given him over the angels to convince them to follow him to a supposed ascension to God's throne. We can first determine that Satan used gossip to draw away the angels because his conversations of futile aspiration were held away from the presence of God, judging by his use of the word *ascend* in Isaiah 14:14. To speak of ascending or going up to the place where God is would mean that at the point of Satan's speaking, he was not where God was. Furthermore, we can determine that gossip was used because in order for the angels to have followed him, he had to have convinced them that the job God was doing was inadequate and he (Satan) could do a better job.

I also submit that this gossip took place over a substantial period of time because faith cometh by hearing, and hearing and hearing continually (Rom. 10:17), even faith in the wrong thing. Satan must have gone on and on with his campaign against God to develop the angels' faith in himself because I'm convinced it would have taken more than a single mention of such a lofty undertaking to convince any number of angels to leave the auspices of the Almighty. With this reasoning, I take the safe theological stance that this first (because it was pre-Adamic) recorded sin of gossip caused the eventual falling away of a third of the heavenly beings.

James 1:15 says: "Then when lust hath conceived, it bringeth forth sin: and sin, when it is *finished*, bringeth forth death" (emphasis mine). This is the general scheme of the account we just overviewed of gossip's conception. Satan began lusting after the Ruler of the universe's position; then sin was born. Satan's ultimate destiny of eternal death, spoken of in James1:15, has yet to come because the age of sin isn't *finished*, but everything he does in this sin dispensation is driven by his hate of God and, subsequently, his hate for us. It's understandable why he hates God, but why does he hate us? We were created in God's likeness. This means we look like him. Whether this means we mirror His triune being (God the Father, God the Son, and God the Holy Ghost) as man the body, man the soul, and man the spirit (Heb. 4:12) or that we in some way resemble whatever aesthetics God may have, we do not know. In whatever way we are in God's likeness, Satan knows (because he spent his life in God's presence), and it drives Satan to hate us. Satan is like a hateful, divorced woman raising the children she had with her ex-husband. She mistreats the children because every look at the children reminds her of their father.

Since Satan cannot defeat God, he seeks to destroy who reminds him of God: us. He hates that God is love, so he drives wedges of confusion among brethren. He hates our outward reflection of the Godhead, so he seeks to destroy the family. And more importantly (for the purpose of this book's theme), he hates God's expression of holiness through our example to the world, so he sows slander. How? Through willing and inadvertent vessels.

In John 8:44, Jesus tells the Pharisees, "Ye are of your father the devil, and the lusts of your father ye will do. He was a murderer from the beginning...." Jesus states explicitly that you can count yourself among the number of Satan's children if you are a murderer. Upon seeing the word *murder*, I'm sure most minds immediately think of the forced cessation of one's life by another. Let's broaden our definition of the word by the standard of the Bible. "Whosoever hateth his brother is a murderer" (1 John 3:15). One might say I have never hated anyone. Proverbs 10:18 teaches if you've ever lied on your brother, hatred hides in your heart. So, although most people would resist the tag *murderer* because they've never physically murdered anyone, when they slander an individual, they are propelled by the exact same characteristic that causes someone to physically murder: hate.

Recap: If you gossip, you operate in hate (Prov. 10:18). If you operate in hate, you're a murderer (1 John 3:15), and if you're a murderer, according to Jesus, you are a child of Satan's.

But in 1 John 3:15, John doesn't conclude his discourse with the harsh talk of murder—he finishes it up with hope by saying no murderer has eternal life *abiding in him*. How is that hopeful? Look closer. Nowhere in the scripture does John allude to this absence of life as being final. Although eternal life does not currently reside in the murderer, that doesn't mean that it can't. Redemption is available even to the murderer. John 3:16 says: "For God so loved the *world* (sinners, e.g., murderers) that He gave his only begotten Son, that *whosoever* (sinners, e.g., murderers) believeth in him should not perish, but have everlasting life" (emphasis mine). Eternal life is available; keep reading.

CHAPTER 2

A DIABOLIC PLAN

One of the three Greek words for gossip is *diabolos,* from which we get our English word *diabolic.* The word alone conjures feelings of fear. The concept is appropriately termed for how diabolic the plan of the enemy is. Satan's plan for gossip is to use people to do just what the word *diabolic* implies: be extremely evil (Luke 6:45). This word study should be enough to sway the Christian from participating in gossip. But let's delve deeper into the diabolic plot of the enemy.

In the last chapter, we discovered that we were created in the likeness of God, which means we look like God, and for this reason, Satan hates us. But we were also created in God's image, which means we have the capacity to act like God. So, if Satan hates us because we look like God, he abhors us when we act like Him, promulgating love, peace, kindness, mercy, etc. So, Satan wants the Christian dead. Not only physically—he'll settle for death of any kind. His agenda is plainly stated in John 10:10: "The thief cometh not, but for to steal, and to kill, and to destroy. . . . " But the sundry ways by which he executes these diabolic schemes may not be quite so evident at first glance. From heaven to the Garden of Eden and even now, Satan doesn't operate blatantly. The Bible calls him subtle (Gen. 3:1, 2 Cor. 11:3).

For example, in Matthew 17:14–18, a man brings his son to Jesus to have demons cast out of the boy. The father tells the Lord sometimes the boy falls into fire and at other times in water. Now to some people, this may seem like plain maniacal behavior, but one who knows the disposition of demons understands that the boy wasn't just falling into the elements—the demons were casting the boy into fire and water to kill him.

Then, another time, in Matthew 8:28–34, Jesus encounters a man on the coast of Gadara living in the graveyard. He was cutting himself with stones. Again, this was not merely psychopathic behavior. The demons that possessed this man were trying to get him to drain the very life source from his body—blood—in effect killing him, for the life of a man is in his blood (Gen. 9:4).

Satan didn't just want the people in the scriptures possessed, as possession was just a means to an end: death. In the same way, the Devil uses gossip as a tool to kill the believer. Yes, gossip can be an agent of death. 1 Corinthians 10:10 warns us, "Neither murmur ye, as some of them also murmured, and were destroyed of the destroyer." Scripture teaches that death comes in two fundamental forms—spiritual and natural—and gossip can lead to both.

First, we'll deal with spiritual death. Constant sin leads to a state of reprobation. A reprobate is one whom God has given innumerable chances, but they insist on sin; therefore, God gives them over to their vile affections. In laymen's terms, God washes his hands of them (Rom. 1:24–32). In the latter portions of Romans 1, numbered among homosexuality and God hating as sins that lead to reprobation are also gossip, slander, and lies. The state of reprobation leads to demonic possession because demons need a barren place to reside (Matt. 12:42–45), and there is no more barren a place than that of a reprobate. Once demons are the occupant of a person, they are considered dead to God (Prov. 21:16, Ezek. 18:4). So, the sin of gossip and the like leads to the state of reprobation, which leads to demonic possession, which is in the eyes of God spiritual death. Therefore, death by the sin of gossip is a possibility.

Now on to natural death. There are hundreds—nay, thousands—of stories across the world of spouses who have heard rumors of their counterparts' unfaithfulness, and in rage kill their spouses and sometimes the spouse's lover as well. There are even stories in the news during the writing of this book of adolescents taking their lives because of rampant rumors spread around their schools about their lifestyles, perceived or actual. And yet again, the Devil succeeds in his plan to kill by way of gossip.

Deeper insight into the sullying strategies of Satan can be found in the church, of all places. The reason gossip is so prevalent in the church is because of the church's makeup. The church is a body of ex-everything—ex-thieves, ex-prostitutes, ex-drug dealers, etc.—and the past lives of these Christians mixed with their current struggles are rife with gossip material. So, Satan, the accuser of the brethren (Rev. 12:10), monopolizes off of it. Because he is so familiar with the church culture, Satan puts gossip under the guise of just sharing so others know how to pray for an individual. This is the oldest trick in the proverbial book. Satan's objective in this is to cause offense, thereby causing disunity among the brethren and in so doing, destroying the church, because he knows that a kingdom divided against itself shall not stand (Matt. 12:25). When we speak of Satan's objective of destroying the church, it is just that: an objective. Of course, we know that he cannot destroy the Universal body, per se. Jesus said that the gates of hell shall not prevail against the church (Matt. 16:18). But Satan can use us within the church to destroy the local church and, in so doing, weaken the Universal Church.

Yet another of Satan's diabolic plans through gossip is to lead the Christian down other avenues of sin. Proverbs 14:12 says: "There is a way which seemeth right unto a man, but the end thereof are the ways of death." Notice the scripture says there's a way, singular. But that way leads to ways, plural. The scripture gives the impression that there is a logical progression to this death. It may start out innocently enough but then gets out of hand. My grandmother would say if you'll lie, you'll steal; if you'll steal, you'll cheat; and if you'll cheat, you'll kill. As a child, I paid little attention to the saying, but in subsequent years, social psychologists have borne witness to it. Their studies prove that criminals begin small, then gradually move on to more serious crimes. In the same way, if a person doesn't take care of their gossiping struggle, sooner or later, they'll find themselves exaggerating and eventually outright lying. Satan is never satisfied; he always wants you to go a little further. Just ask King David.

In 2 Samuel 11, during the time he was supposed to be at war, David woke up one morning at home and went to his window. There, he saw a beautiful woman named Bathsheba bathing. Okay, these aren't so bad—there's no sin in taking a break from your military responsibilities for whatever reason or happening upon Bathsheba taking a bath in his window's view. Since they're not quite sins yet, the Bible would call these weights (Heb. 12:1). But David did not unfix his gaze so as to lust after Bathsheba. There goes sin number one: he lusted after this woman. David enquired about the woman and found out that she was married but sent for her anyway. When Bathsheba came to David, he had sex with her. There goes sin number two: David committed adultery. Some time had passed, and Bathsheba sent word to David that she was pregnant. David abused his power as king and called Bathsheba's husband, Uriah, from battle for a supposed vacation so he would lie with his wife and think the baby Bathsheba was pregnant with belonged to him. There goes sin number three: David sought to deceive Uriah. But Uriah, being loyal to the king, refused to go home and enjoy his wife while his fellow soldiers fought on the battlefield. So, David devised another plan. He sent Uriah back to war but this time placed him on the front line of battle to be killed. There goes sin number four: David was now guilty of murder. And it all started with one sin that started with one weight—just one.

Finally, if the enemy fails at every other attempt to steal from, kill, and destroy the believer with gossip, he'll use his principle tool: lies. The Bible calls the Devil the Father of lies (John 8:44), and he does it well; he's had thousands of years of practice. He does it in such a way that the lie sounds more believable than the truth itself.

The first example that comes to mind is Joseph in Genesis 39:1–23. A high official in Egypt named Potiphar made Joseph the manager of all that he owned. While Joseph would be working, Potiphar's wife would make sexual advances to Joseph, but Joseph would deny her. One day, when Joseph was in the house alone with Potiphar's wife, she grabbed him by the clothes and made another advance. Joseph was so shaken that he ran away from her and left his clothes in her hands. Potiphar's wife was so upset that Joseph wouldn't give in to her that she told her husband that Joseph tried to lie with her and presented Joseph's clothes as proof. Potiphar and everyone else believed the seductress's story because it appeared to be true. And Joseph went to jail because of it. All because of a lie that looked true.

Joseph's story reminds me of a conversation I had some time ago. In the conversation, I was trying to defend the reputation of a friend against an allegation I knew was false but seemed true. While defending my friend, the person I was having the conversation with used the antiquated adage, "Where there is smoke, there is fire." Which is to say if it looks like it, it must be so. When the person made the statement, my immediate response was, "If I had a battery-operated smoke machine or the combination of dry ice and water, I could prove to you that fire is not necessary to produce smoke." In other words, things aren't always the way they seem. People can produce an ill impression of someone based on the way things look, like Potiphar's wife did to Joseph.

The reason the Devil uses this kind of trickery with people's perceptions of others is yet another diabolical plan of his. He knows that if our perceptions about someone is wrong, we could make decisions that cause us to miss out on our greatest blessings or fall into our worst despair. For example, after that encounter I had in the introduction of this book with those ministers in college, I could never look at the preachers they talked about the same. Every time I watched them on TV, my mind would be preoccupied with what I had heard about them rather than listening to what they had to say, and they could very well have had a specific word from God for me. But I'll never know, because gossip warped my perception of them.

New Methods

Satan, ever the opportunist, has even adapted gossip to the technological age. I do not subscribe to the belief that the Internet is evil, but forums that allow people to make public, sensitive information or disparaging statements about other individuals anonymously are evil. The cowardly Christians who indulge in gossip and slander online do so under the false security that it's not "really" gossiping. Doesn't that justification sound familiar? Satan deceived Eve with similar semantics when enticing her with the forbidden fruit: "You shall not 'surely' die" (Gen. 3:4). But word games don't fool God. Let me assure you, even when it's typed, it's gossip, and mandate will be brought on it. Can you believe that the Bible has something to say about online gossip? We learned earlier that the sin of gossip begins in the heart, and in Matthew 15:19–20, Jesus says, "For out of the heart proceed evil thoughts, murders (plural, so gossip is included), thefts, false witness, blasphemies: These are the things which defile a man. . . . " So, if it's conceived in the mind and emanates from your person, whether by fingers, mouth, eyes, etc., God holds you responsible for it. You're not guiltless just because man can't see you, as "the eyes of the Lord run to and fro throughout the whole earth" (2 Chron. 16:9).

To help thwart the diabolic plan of the enemy to tarnish your reputation, abstain from the very appearance of evil (1 Thess. 5:22). You may not be doing anything wrong, but stay away from situations that may make you look like you could be doing wrong. This may not be fail-proof, but it certainly lessens the chances of reputation damage. To thwart the diabolic plan of the enemy to use you as a gossip agent, *don't do it* (Lev. 19:16)! No explanation needed. Just don't do it—God said so.

CHAPTER 3

MORE THAN WORDS

Words are not just language. They are divine. King Solomon says in Proverbs 18:21, "Death and life are in the power of the tongue. . . . " That small muscle in your mouth isn't so small after all. In the beginning, God created the very world with words. The law of first mention says the way something begins is the pattern for which it will continue. So, whether we know it or not, our lives are governed by our words because that's the way life as we know it began. But there are some who contend that we "word-of-faith people" make too much ado over words. To them, I say, "You don't put gas in a car initially and decide later that you can put water in the tank. If the car took gas in the beginning, the car will take gas forever. The same with life—since it was created by words, it must be sustained by the same." So we would be wise to take painstaking measures to guard our speech because just like your words have the ability to bring good things, careless and slanderous words can be used to bring destruction, devastation, and even death, literally.

According to the Israelites' law, two witnesses were necessary to bring an allegation against a person (Deut. 17: 6). But there were apparently those who still brought false accusations against others, evident by the need for God to include this commandment in the Decalogue. In accordance with the law, if a person was condemned to death by stoning, the people who brought the accusation were required to place their hand on the head of the condemned to indicate their responsibility in the consequential death of this person. If the accusers were found to have borne false witness against the person in question, they would suffer the penalty that would have been doled out to the person they falsely accused. Though we are no longer constrained by the law (Gal. 5:18, Rom. 6:14), it is still good (Ps. 19:7–8, Rom. 7:12). So persons who bear false witness against another will not escape reprimand, for: "These six things doth the Lord hate; yea, seven are an abomination unto him: . . . A lying tongue . . . A false witness that speaketh lies, and he that soweth discord among brethren" (Prov. 6:16, 19).

Prayerfully, now you see that our words affect absolutely everything. In the case that you need further proof, just think about it: You were saved by your confession. Your marriage was legitimized by your vows, and in some cases, persons have verbally instructed family members and physicians not to place them on life support, in effect ending their lives with their words. Words are a law, and like the law of gravity, everyone is affected by it, even unbelievers. Unbelievers condemn themselves because of their lack of confession to salvation (Matt. 12:34–37), but Christians are judged on earth for wrong confession (e.g., lying, gossip, etc.) (1 Cor. 3:13–15).

Let's see some of the effects that a Christian's wrong confession can produce.

Marqui Antwon W. Taylor

How Gossip Affects Your Mind

Paul tells the church at Rome in Romans 12:2, "And be not conformed to this world: but be ye transformed by the renewing of your mind." This scripture lets me know that it is the responsibility of the believer to keep his own mind, not God, as is traditionally believed. This quality is what sets us apart from all other creation: our will. God has given humans the unique ability to disagree with and even deny Him. As powerful as the Holy Ghost is, he cannot operate in the life of an individual without them having a made-up mind to grant him access (Mark 6:5). If the Holy Ghost is an obsolete variable in someone's life, that person gives control of their mind over to sin.

One whose mind is controlled by sin is capable of all manner of wickedness, gossip included. Gossip makes the mind insensitive to fellow man. It's sort of like the experience soldiers have at war. Under normal circumstances, they would never be able to stomach killing someone, but in war, they separate themselves from the humanity in the other person to kill them. The listener of gossip is not exempt; they fall prey to the same insensitivity (Prov. 18:8). If the gossiper is a murderer, then the listener of gossip steps over the corpse of the recently killed without any regard.

The cunning Satan knows the mind is his main access point into a person's life, so his desire is to get people to believe his suggestions, after which he can control their perceptions, and if he controls their perceptions, he can control their actions. Again with Mama's wisdom: she would say if you give him an inch, he'll take a mile. The enemy is merciless, and once he has control of a person's actions, there is no place to go but down. The person becomes consumed with transgression. Example:

"And when it was day, certain of the Jews banded together, and bound themselves under a curse saying that they would neither eat nor drink till they had killed Paul" (Acts 23:12).

The scripture begins by saying "when it was day," which means what they were going to do was going to be done even if everyone could see it. Their vitriol outweighed whatever shame they would have otherwise felt. The scripture continues to explain that these men came together to destroy Paul, so not only does misery like company, but misery prefers the company of family because destroying is the agenda of Satan. And these men were of Satan's brood because Jesus did say that if you do Satan's work, he is your father (John 8:44). The Bible continues that the men were so unyielding in their mission that they bound themselves under a curse that they wouldn't eat or drink until it was accomplished. Anyone who becomes so devoted to the purpose of the demise of another person that their own life takes a back seat is definitely consumed by sin and has no part with the Father. These religious men, mind you, voluntarily placed themselves under a curse "until. . . . " How dangerous. The risk that's taken when one binds themselves under a curse is that they may die while still under it, and the end of any curse is hell (Matt. 25:41).

Do you see now why gossip isn't so innocent? All the Devil needs is a small foothold, something seemingly as small as gossip, to destroy lives, the perpetrator, and the victim.

How Gossip Affects Your Faith

Gossip not only has the potential to ruin other's lives but to hinder your own. Hate and love are considered absolutes, which mean they can't coexist. It is impossible to hate someone while loving them at the same time. The enemy knows this, so he sets traps for you in the form of opportunities to gossip. When you do, you operate in hate; therefore, your faith is blocked. For example, if a well-studied person operates in faith by confessing God's word of protection, wealth, healing, etc., over their life and the lives of their family every day but also gossips, the sin of gossip cancels out the confessions of faith. Remember, love is inactive when hate is in operation, and when one gossips, they operate in hate. The Bible says, "Faith works by Love" (Gal. 5:6). In other words, faith is the car, but love is the gasoline. You can sit in the car all day, but if you don't have the fuel, you're not going anywhere.

Furthermore, confession is a form of prayer, and gossip a form of iniquity. Psalms 66:18 tells us that if we regard iniquity in our heart, God will not hear our prayers.

How Gossip Affects Your Anointing

The anointing is the burden removing yoke destroying power of God (Isa. 10:26). It helps us operate in our call effectively. Though gifts and callings are without repentance (Rom. 11:29), the anointing is on loan from God. The loan of the anointing is predicated upon love. 1 Corinthians 13:1–13 teaches that God doesn't even acknowledge a person who isn't walking in love, so it's absurd to think that He would lend his anointing to someone operating in hate by gossiping. But I was guilty of such thinking.

For a long time, I would gossip and still have command of a church while ministering in Word or song, so I was under the false impression that I was all right with God. But I began to notice that ministering became increasingly harder and harder. There was one speaking engagement in particular where it was glaringly evident that I stood alone, without efficacy of the Spirit. When someone ministers under the anointing, it's the anointing doing the work, not the person, but when they're ministering in a backslidden condition as I was, the anointing lifts because it's sin-sensitive. So, I found myself attempting to manufacture a feeling for the people by my own power. In essence, what I was doing was killing people through the week via the hate of gossip, then trying to spiritually resuscitate those same folks through song during praise and worship on Sunday morning.

If you have an issue with a sister or brother or even if you know they have an issue with you, Jesus tells us in Matthew 5:23–24 to save our gifts, reconcile with the person, then come back and offer those gifts to the Lord. Has your ministry been suffering lately? Check your relationships with others because your relationship with God depends on your relationship with those around you (1 John 4:20).

Marqui Antwon W. Taylor

How Gossip Affects Your Witness

Thou that makest thy boast of the law, through breaking the law dishonourest thou God? For the name of God is blasphemed among the Gentiles through you, as it is written.
—Romans 2:23–24

Paul tells these religious men of Rome: though you know the law better than anyone else, it is you who transgress the law worse than anyone else. It takes pride of exorbitant amounts to know the Word and the consequences of disobeying it and totally ignore them. After reading the scriptures and/or this book, if when you get to heaven you are confronted with your gossiping, you are without excuse.

I was in a store once and struck up a conversation with a middle-aged lady. Before we went our separate ways, I tried to veer the conversation toward an introduction to Christ. When the woman sensed what I was doing, she stopped me in my tracks and said, "You're a nice young man, and I enjoyed the conversation up until now, but I know where you're going, and I don't want to hear it. I grew up around church people, and they're a mess. I vowed when I got out of my parents' house that I would never step foot in a church again." This seems to be the general consensus among many in society. If you ask any person who doesn't attend church services regularly why they don't, they will undoubtedly tell you that it's because church people have the reputation of being hypocritical. They have been around enough church folk to know that they talk to you, then turn around and talk about you. I believe this is why the church misses out on some of the greatest minds ever. If these people were to ever come to Christ, they would promote the kingdom agenda better than anyone, but they use their gifts in the world because they're disillusioned with the church.

The Hindu-born Mahatma Gandhi is credited with saying, "I would have become a Christian had I first not met Christians." If the world sees us avoid the seemingly small sin of gossip, they'll take our faith as a more seriously.

In Romans 2:24, Paul makes one of the strongest statements in the entire Bible; he tells these men that it's because of them that God has a bad name among the unbelievers. The word *blasphemed* Paul uses in the scriptures is translated *slandered*. Sounds familiar, doesn't it? This is the exact thing that got Satan kicked out of Heaven: slandering God. So, these men in Romans are the children of Satan because remember, Jesus said, "The lusts of your father ye will do" (John 8:44). Can you imagine at the judgment God saying to you, "Someone decided against coming to Christ because they heard you maligning the reputation of someone already in the church"? Consider it; it can happen.

CHAPTER 4

BUT IT'S TRUE

Satan isn't called the "arch deceiver" for no reason. It has been said that his greatest deception is to convince people that he doesn't exist. I believe that a greater deception is his doctrine of graded sin. Graded sin is the belief that there is a hierarchy of sin, and down through the years, gossip has been placed so low on the list that it's almost not considered a sin anymore. Self-righteousness propels the allegiance to this incorrect doctrine. The logic behind graded sin is if your sin is worse than mine, then mine must not be so bad. I call this pseudo-holiness; it's all about magnifying your sin to minimize mine. But these pseudo-holy individuals would do well to remember that the only difference in their sin and the person's sin they're gossiping about is that the person being gossiped about got caught. It could have very well been the other way around if not for grace. To these self-righteous ones, the Bible says in the Epistle of James 2:10, "For whosoever shall keep the whole law, and yet offend in one point, he is guilty of all." So, if you're not an adulterer, you're a thief who lies on tax returns; if you're not a thief, you're a glutton who can't say no to another plate. My point is there is no little sin or big sin; sin is sin. Remember, it's sin to discuss someone else's sin for the purpose of entertainment or self aggrandizement.

But for the sake of tuition, let's go with the premise that what's being said about someone is true. Is it then all right to repeat it? Absolutely not—it's still slander. In the Old Testament, slander is defined as the giving of a bad report with the purpose of damaging the reputation of a person, even if it's true.

Numbers 12:1-2 says: "1 And Miriam and Aaron spoke against Moses because of the Ethiopian woman whom he had married; for he had married an Ethiopian woman. 2 And they said, Hath the Lord spoken only by Moses? hath he also not spoken by us? And the Lord heard it."

So far, we see that what has been said about Moses is true, but it's slander. In verse number one, the phrase "spoke against" makes it clear that the purpose for which the statement was made was to discredit Moses.

Numbers 12:9-10 continues: "9 And the anger of the Lord was kindled against them; and he departed. 10 And the cloud departed from off the tabernacle and, behold, Miriam became leprous, white as snow: and Aaron looked upon Miriam, and, behold, she was leprous."

The sin is seeming more and more serious, isn't it? God deemed it so serious that he struck Miriam (Moses's sister, no less) with leprosy, the most feared disease of the day. Miriam had difficulty with the fact that Moses had sinned in the flesh by marrying an African, but she overlooked the fact that she was sinning in the spirit: assassination by gossip. Just like two wrongs don't make a right, two sins don't make one righteous. Though what Miriam was sharing with Aaron was true, it still required punishment.

Truth alone does not license the sharing of unnecessary information about someone. The difference between gossip and sharing concern isn't whether or not it's true but the intention behind the sharing. The place that Miriam was sharing from was a place of jealousy (Num. 12:2).

I call people like Miriam "mess tour guides" because it takes a mental individual to prefer hanging around a pile of someone else's mess (use your imagination). Since it was against the custom of Jews to marry outside their religion, Miriam found this offense against Moses disgusting and took Aaron to the perceived filth—much like people today who make it their business to take everyone they meet back to the place where you might have made a mess. It matters not to them that you have since received forgiveness and that both you and God have forgotten it (Ps. 103:11–12). They will always remember when. Don't be a "mess tour guide" because if you hang around mess long enough, you'll begin to smell like it.

Whose Truth?

A group of people and I were watching a news telecast that reported the tragic drowning of two people in a river that is the only access to a secluded island community in South Carolina. The residents of the island had years earlier refused an offer from some developers to build a bridge from the city to their little island. Sometime before this tragedy had occurred, I had watched a public television documentary that explained the situation. The reason the residents refused the bridge was because they would not be able to use the bridge but for ambulance emergencies and for funeral processions with permission. Furthermore, the development of the bridge would cause the residents' property taxes to skyrocket and would greatly impact the integrity of the simple living that the island is known for.

After the news anchor reported the story of the drowning, he mentioned that the residents of the island had refused a bridge some years earlier but offered no more information than that. Someone in the room with me where I was watching this very abruptly exclaimed, "How stupid, a bridge could have saved those people's lives!" Immediately, I understood how easily perceptions are shaped. This incident taught me that incomplete information is just as dangerous as misinformation, and speaking without all the facts is most unwise (Prov. 11:9). Anyone else with the limited information the news anchor offered would have felt the same way the person in the room with me did, but the truth of the news anchor was not all the truth there was.

Sometimes we have to deal with the truth of some spooky person's dream or vision (Jer. 23:28). Understand that although some dreams do come from God, not all do. Dreams must be measured by the monolith of God's Word. Dreams can come from any number of things: the last thing you were thinking of before going to sleep, chemicals released in the brain triggered by something eaten, or according to Ecclesiastes 1:53, a result of being too busy. When it is indeed God who has given a word of wisdom to someone in a dream, it is never to be shared with anyone other than the subject of the dream unless instructed otherwise. But God will likely never give these kinds of dreams or insight to a known gossip because He is not the author of confusion (1 Cor. 14:33). Once a pastor shared with me a dream that he had about me, and I won't say that he didn't have the dream, but if I did believe that it was from God, he ruined his credibility when I found out he shared the dream with someone else. Besides that, the dream was totally off anyway. But there is a way to determine "the" truth from someone else's truth.

One would think that truth is just truth across the board. Oh, if it were just that simple. It has been said in a recount of an ordeal between two persons that there is person A's truth on one side, person B's truth on the other, and "the" truth in the middle. For this reason, at the founding of America, the founding fathers set up an ingenious system of checks and balances in which a judge and sometimes peers could decipher as best they could the truth from evidence and testimony presented to them. And though this system of justice may not work 100 percent of the time, it is one of the best ways to make determinations in disputes. But there is a spiritual way that is fail-proof in determining what is "the" truth in any given situation every time: utilize the Spirit of truth available to you. Our human abilities are limited, so there are times when it will be impossible for us to determine whether or not something is true, but isn't it good to know that God freely offers us his discerning power and it's available for the asking?

The Correct Response to Gossip

Realistically speaking, the reputations of some are going to be marred because of their own foolish indiscretion, and in this case, what is your responsibility if any at all? Galatians 6:1–2 says: "Brethren, if a man be overtaken in a fault, ye which are spiritual, restore such an one in the spirit of meekness; considering thyself, lest thou also be tempted. Bear ye one another's burdens, and so fulfil the law of Christ." We know that the law of Christ is love, and love, according to Proverbs 13:10, dictates that you give Godly counsel to the person concerning their particular situation. But what is discussed should never leave the room you all were conversing in (Matt. 18:15). In such a scenario, my grandmother would say, "Learn to seal your lips."

We often make the mistake of believing because someone brings us "choice" information about someone else, they trust us, when in reality they unconsciously think of you as a trash can to dump other people's garbage in. The moment you put your foot down and tell them, "I don't want to hear the gossip," they'll begin to see you in a different light. They'll see you as a respectable, no-nonsense person. And who knows, you may influence them to stop gossiping altogether. Also consider if they'll gossip to you about someone else, they'll gossip about you to someone else.

"Oh, be careful little Christian what you do. Oh, be careful little Christian what you do, for the Father up above is looking down below. Oh, be careful little Christian what you do." That's a verse in a song I used to sing in the Sunbeam choir at my church as a child. Though the song was supposed to foster Christian behavior in children, its message is one that all believers should live by. It would seem like such a simple message would be redundant to an adult, but it is said that members of the Christian army are the only soldiers that kick fellow soldiers while they're already down. This sad commentary is the exact opposite of the grace that our Lord and example exhibited while here on earth. Every opportunity that a Christian can grasp to really demonstrate true Christian behavior, they should do so and not resort to their old sinful nature.

CHAPTER 5

THE GRAPEVINE

The Devil does not have creative power—he has never and will never create anything. All he can do is pervert what already exists. That's why the image Jesus uses to define the Christian life, the devil uses as a massive tool of corruption: the infamous grapevine. Let's deal with Satan's faulty analogy of the grapevine first.

One of the three Greek words for Gossip is *psithurismos*, which means to whisper. This Greek word is where the "psst" gesture to get someone's attention comes from; this signaling has always sounded sinister to me. Nothing good normally comes after a "psst." In fact, Proverbs 16:28 and Romans 1:29 speak of the dangers of a whisperer. So, be leery of something being told to you in a whispering manner.

The best example of Satan's grapevine is a game we used to play in summer camp called telephone. The format of the game is to sit all participants next to one another in a circle. The game begins with someone whispering a statement in the ear of their immediate neighbor, and that neighbor whispers what they heard to the next neighbor, and so on. The premise of the game was to try to get the original message to the last person in the group. I have never witnessed or heard of any group that has ever finished the game with the same message it started with. If it is virtually unachievable to keep the integrity of a small statement with persons in matter of minutes, how much more impossible is it when the message spans days and sometimes years?

The Center for Disease Control has found that most alcoholics start drinking because of some life hardship or personal struggle. It is my theory that that's the same reason Christians overindulge in the gossip grapevine. There is some personal fault in their own life that they wish to forget, which makes them indulge in the affairs of others. But one grape isn't enough to make a person inebriated; in fact, neither can a day's worth of eating grapes make a person drunk. The fermenting process is what does the damage. The time one spends in other's dealings is what makes all the difference in the world.

The difference in socially drinking and being a drunk is not much different than Hebrews 12:1's contrast between a weight and a sin. A weight is anything that diverts your attention from God, like overhearing disparaging comments about someone. Sin is defined as missing the mark or actually engaging in the gossiping conversation. It is interesting to me that the last of the Greek words for gossip is *phluarus,* which means to babble, and anyone who has been around a drunk person for any length of time will tell you that talking nonsense is characteristic of a drunk. But their inebriation does not exempt them from consequence. For example, if the drunk in question gets behind the wheel of a car, they will not be spared because they're drunk—they will be arrested. In the same way, an excessive gossiper does not have exemption from the penalty of their foolish words. "But I say unto you, that every idle word that men shall speak, they shall give an account thereof in the day of judgment" (Matt. 12:36).

There is something to be said about the fact that a grapevine cannot stand alone; it must be supported by a network of posts, nails, and wire. The truth can stand on its own. More often than not, the person relaying information in this slanderous network called a grapevine is based solely on hearsay. It is for this reason that this "grapevine" should be deemed totally unreliable and have no right among the Christian community.

Now let's look at Jesus's application of the vine in John 15:1–2, 5–8:

> 1 I am the true vine, and my father is the husbandman. 2 Every branch that beareth not fruit he taketh away: and every branch that beareth fruit, he purgeth it, that it may bring forth more fruit. . . . 5 I am the vine, ye are the branches. He that abideth in me, and I in him, the same bringeth forth much fruit: for without me ye can do nothing. 6 If a man abide not in me, he is cast forth as a branch, and is withered; and men gather them and cast them into the fire, and they are burned. 7 If ye abide in me, and my words abide in you, ye shall ask what you will, and it shall be done unto you. 8 Herein is my Father glorified, that ye bear much fruit; so shall ye be my disciples.

First of all, let's not relegate fruit in this scripture to just new converts as is common. The scripture could very plausibly be referring to good works. Galatians 5: 22 lists different good works and calls them *fruit* of the spirit. Also, in Titus 3:14, it says, "And let ours learn to maintain *good works* for necessary uses, that they be not *unfruitful*" (emphasis mine). So what Christ did when he gave this discourse on the vine was establish the right concept of the Christian's role in their relation with other people, and go figure, it doesn't involve gossip like Satan's ill-applied grapevine. In fact, verse six speaks of those who don't exhibit good works but bad or indifferent works, and Jesus says of these people men shall cast them into fire. There are theologians who subscribe to the belief that this fire is not referring to being cast into the physical hell. Likely because they interpret the word *fruit* in the scripture to mean new converts and think it's a stretch that God would send someone to hell for not being responsible for bringing people into the kingdom. On the grounds that I believe the word *fruit* in the scripture refers to good works, it stands to reason that hell would be the destination of those who don't have good works (James 2:17–18). Moreover, among the many scriptures that support the latter, there is Matthew 13:38–39, which says, "The field is the world; the good seed are the children of the kingdom; but the tares are the children of the wicked one; The enemy that sowed them is the devil; the harvest is the end of the world; and the reapers are the angels." Side note: There is no discrepancy in Jesus's use of the word *men* in John that will cast the unfruitful into fire and his use of the word *angels* in Matthew because the Bible frequently refers to angels as "men" or "sons of God."

Jesus concludes his discourse of the vine by saying that if you abide in me and bear much fruit, the Father is glorified. So, the real application of the grapevine is to demonstrate that if we live by the teachings of Christ in doing good works rather than practicing sin, we can make God smile. Now who wouldn't want that?

CHAPTER 6

JUDGMENT

Romans 2:1–3 reads: "1 Therefore thou art inexcusable, O man, whosoever thou art that judgest: for wherin thou judgest another, thou condemnest thyself; for thou that judgest doest the same things. 2 But we are sure that the judgment of God is according to truth against them which commit such things. 3 And thinkest thou this, O man, that judgest them which do such things, and doest the same, that thou escape the judgment of God?"

It is impossible to speak about gossip and not speak about the element of judgment that it has. When we gossip, we subconsciously believe that the person we're talking about deserves the punishment of our gossip, thereby making ourselves judges. The word *judge* used in the scripture is originally *krino,* which means *to condemn finally.* James 4:12 says, "There is one lawgiver, who is able to save and to destroy: who art thou that judgest another?" How dare we attempt to take the position of God? We can barely conduct our mortal lives appropriately. God has a purpose for everything he commands of us, and the reason he instructs us not to judge is because He knows that no matter how self-assured we believe ourselves to be, we can't handle the job of judge or its consequences. What consequences? Verse one says that when we judge another for anything, we are guilty of the same thing we judged them for. As an ardent studier of the scriptures, I am never satisfied with the English translation alone. I make it a practice to read the King James version of a scripture first, then compare it to its original language. So after I read verse one of the King James version, I was certain it didn't mean if I judged someone for lying that I myself became a liar. How wrong I was. After studying the original text, I found that that is exactly what the scripture means. So, however dastardly the sin is that you judge in another, is how dastardly you are yourself. This is what Jesus meant when he told us not to judge lest we ourselves be judged (Matt. 7:1).

Accordingly, in becoming partaker of another person's sin, you must also become partaker of God's reprimand on that sin. So, if God's mandate for that person's sin is the loss of a job, you may well be receiving a pink slip shortly. Proverbs 21:23 says, "Whoso keepeth his mouth and his tongue keepeth his soul from troubles."

In all this talk about judgment, I don't want anyone to get the wrong idea. If your leader, a close friend, or a well-meaning family member confronts you about some sin or indiscretion in your life, they're not judging you. Remember, judgment is assuming something about someone. A friend, leader, or family member is around you most and knows you best, so they don't have to make assumptions—they're just calling a spade a spade. Or, according to Jesus, they're calling an apple an apple. He said in Matthew 7:16 that they shall know you by the fruit that you bear.

It's easy to say that you don't judge, but let's see how easy it really is to slip into the sin of judgment.

2 Samuel 12:1–7 reads:

> 1 And the Lord sent Nathan unto David. And he came unto him, and said unto him, There were two men in one city; the one rich, and the other poor. 2 The rich man had exceeding many flocks and herds: 3 But the poor man had nothing, save one little ewe lamb, which he had bought and nourished up: and it grew up together with him, and with his children; it did eat of his own meat, and drank his own cup, and lay in his bosom, and was unto him as a daughter. 4 And there came to him a traveler unto the rich man, and he spared to take his own flock and of his own herd, to dress for the wayfaring man that was come unto him; but took the poor man's lamb, and dressed it for the man that was come to him. 5 And David's anger was greatly kindled against the man; and he said to Nathan as the Lord liveth, the man that has done this thing shall surely die: 6 And he shall restore the lamb fourfold, because he did this thing, and because he had no pity. 7 And Nathan said to David, Thou art the man. . . .

This story takes modern form with a woman watching her local news channel when a story is reported on a man who tragically murdered someone. The woman goes off on a tangent, yelling at the TV at the top of her lungs, "Send him to the electric chair!" This woman totally ignores the fact that she has also been committing the crime of murder all of her adult life. Her husband left her for another woman twenty years earlier, and the bitterness she harbored toward her ex and his mistress had turned into hate, and hate (we have discovered) is murder. In Matthew 7:5, Jesus scolds, "Thou hypocrite, first cast out the beam out of thine own eye; and then shalt thou see clearly to cast out the mote out of thy brother's eye."

David was guilty of the same in 2 Samuel 12:1–7. He wasn't responding to Nathan's story based on his knowledge of proven facts, but on what he had heard alone. David had no intentions to investigate; his immediate response was, "This man shall surely die." He got what he said; how he judged was how he was judged.

When we judge, we get the false sense that we are being holy, but it's just the opposite: we are really just being foolish. James 1:26–27 says, "If any man among you seem to be religious and bridleth not his tongue, but deceiveth his own heart this man's religion is in vain. Pure religion and undefiled before God and the Father is this, to visit the fatherless and widows in their affliction, and to keep himself unspotted from the world." In other words, you want to look holy? Do good deeds, live right, and leave the judging to God.

CHAPTER 7

DELIVERANCE

Deliverance for the Slanderer

In Alcoholics Anonymous, they make you stand, identify yourself, then identify your vice. This is done because there's no need for deliverance where there is no problem. So, first admit that you have a problem with gossip and that it's not innocent, it's not all right, and it's not mindless chatter—it's wrong. Now the process of deliverance can begin. I specify it as a process because God isn't going to zap it off of you; you've got to walk this deliverance out. The reason is because there is no such thing as a gossiping spirit; this sin is one of will. Galatians 5:19–21 says: "Now the works of the flesh are manifest . . . slanderers . . . murders. . . . " So, there are some practical steps that need to be made for one to be delivered.

1. Perfect your relationship with God – You perfect your relationship with God by spending time with him in prayer and study. Prayer causes you to become sensitive to the things of God. So,

in your daily life, when you're about to do something that would displease Him, that prayer time you had earlier makes you aware of his presence and opt out of sinning. Study of his word will practically let you know the mind of God. "Thou shalt not bear false witness against thy neighbor" (Exod. 20:16).

2. Consider the blessings of holiness – I think for too long the church has tried to scare sin out of people by preaching hellfire and brimstone. This method fails more than it succeeds. In Romans 7, Paul teaches that keeping conscious of sin to prevent indulging in it actually has the opposite effect. Like a child, the more you tell them not to do something, the more they want to do it. This is human nature. I believe that to consider the blessings of holiness is a far better way to keep one on the straight and narrow. Paul seems to agree; he says in Romans 2:4 that it is the goodness of the Lord that leads to repentance, not His wrath. Jesus says, " . . . and he that is holy, let him be holy still. And, behold, I come quickly; and my reward is with me, to give every man according as his work shall be" (Rev. 22:11–12). The eternal reward of holiness far outweighs the momentary satisfaction of slander. Think of that the next time you have the opportunity to gossip.

3. Be considerate of yourself and others – First consider how you would feel if someone had lied on you or shared the most regrettable moment of your life. Consider the potential victim of your gossip. Think beyond whatever gratification you get from gossiping and think about the irreparable damage you could cause

the person for the remainder of their life. Also consider the regret you may later feel.

There is a story told of a young man in the middle ages who confessed to a priest that he had slandered his neighbor. The priest told the young man that he was forgiven. But that didn't satisfy the young man; he wanted to know what he had to do to restore the person he had slandered. The priest told him to go place a feather on the doorstep of every house in the village and when he was done to return to him. After the young man had placed a feather on the doorstep of every house in the village and returned to the priest, he asked the priest with excitement if the neighbor had been restored. The priest told the young man the person would only be restored after he went back to every house in the village and retrieved the feathers. The young man protested, "That's impossible, the wind would have blown them all away by now." The priest then said, "In the same way, it is impossible to restore your neighbors reputation, and you must now live with what you have done to him forever."

4. Stay away from gossiping folk – Proverbs 20:19 says, "He that goeth about as a talebearer revealeth secrets: therefore meddle not with him that flattereth with his lips." Enough said.

Matthew 12:29 reads, "Or else how can one enter a strong man's house, and spoil his goods, except he first bind the strong man?"

You may discover that after walking this thing out, not only will your epic struggle with gossip be conquered, but it will break any other underlining issues you may have had. If you want stop a tree from growing, you don't pick all the fruit off the tree—you cut it at the root. You'll likely find that other proclivities just stop, as they were a subsidiary of your gossiping problem.

The main key to this kind of deliverance is taking back control of the mind. To keep your deliverance, you must keep your mind on Him (Isa. 26:3). This is what the Bible means when it says, "Walk in the spirit, and ye shall not fulfill the lust of the flesh" (Gal. 5:16). As long as you're walking in the spirit (keeping your mind on God), the flesh becomes a non-issue. That's the reason I didn't make *consider the consequences of sin* one of the steps to deliverance in the beginning of this chapter, rather, *consider the blessings of holiness*. The scare tactic methods of preaching have been used for centuries, and for some people, they don't work. Their sin problem persists. I'm persuaded that if some people are taught the benefits of holiness more than the consequences of sin, the flesh will become less difficult to deal with. In theological terms, that's called getting rid of the sin conscience and embracing the righteousness of God through Christ Jesus.

Deliverance for the Slandered

The natural reaction for the unfairly maligned is to ask why. It may just be occasion. The perpetrator may know that there is most often not immediate mandate on the sin of gossip, so they just do it when the opportunity presents itself (Eccles. 8:11). It may be jealousy, it may be retaliation for some perceived wrong done to them, or it may not be ours to know. Everyone's situation is different. But know that the intensity of the enemy's attack against you is always indicative of the threat you pose to the kingdom of darkness. The Devil doesn't waste his time attempting to destroy someone who doesn't have the potential to greatly impact his work. So don't let this experience depress you to the extent that you feel inconsequential in the great scheme of things—it's just the opposite. When you emerge from this debacle, don't give up, but make the Devil and all his demons sorry they ever messed with you. Fulfill God's destiny for your life!

It is important that you do not isolate yourself during your season of slander. Elijah would tell you that this only makes the situation worse (1 Kings 19:4–14). The Devil would love nothing more than to make you think that you have to go through this by yourself. There will be people who God strategically places in your life to offer Godly comfort. Do not shut them out. The emotion of trepidation is an understandable one in your situation, but turn that trepidation into wisdom. Rather than immediately shutting new relationships down, try the spirits of the individuals first through prayer and Spirit-led observation (1 John 4:1). Also, once they've proven loyalty, trust God. Don't subject these new friends to daily FBI clearance tests. A person can only be expected to take so much. Don't let the disloyalty of past relationships sabotage destiny relationships.

There is life after your reputation has been smeared. There is a very famous gospel singer whom I drew encouragement from during my time of trial. This man endured vicious rumors about his lifestyle so much so that it affected his health and cost him his marriage. Some years after suffering through the effects of these character-indicting rumors, the person responsible for the lies publicly apologized and admitted that the rumors were all his fabrications. So there is credence to Proverbs

18:7–8—slander can and has destroyed people's lives. But it doesn't have to. You have a choice. This man chose not to let the rumors destroy him. Today, he is still singing and preaching to the glory of God. Let this testimony encourage you that, no weapon of slander, lies, jealousy, etc., that is formed against you shall prosper, and every tongue that rises against you in judgment you shall condemn (Isa. 54:17).

But this condemnation should not come as acts of retaliation on people. The scripture is clear that you condemn or curse their words and pray for them (Matt. 5:44). If you know where the slander started, do not seek revenge. "Dearly beloved, avenge not yourselves, but rather give place unto wrath; for it is written, Vengeance is mine; I will repay, saith the Lord" (Rom. 12:19). When you get back at your adversaries, you don't allow God to do it, and I'm sure I'll get no arguments that he can do it better. Easier said than done, right? We have a super power to our advantage.

When my son was much younger, I got stuck watching one of his favorite superhero movies with him. While watching it, I became intrigued by one superhero in particular. Her superpower was a force field; it was a clear bubble that nothing and no one could penetrate. She would activate this force field when in conflict with the bad guys. I realized that as Christians, we have a force field too. It's called resistance. Satan fights in the spirit world, and so must we. 2 Corinthians 10:4 says the weapons that are available to us are not natural but spiritual, one of which is found in James 4:7; the force field of resistance. When the urge to strike back comes over you, activate your force field. Keep only the positive in your bubble and the negative out. The latter portion of James 4:7 teaches that our force field of resistance tires the enemy and causes him to retreat.

This spiritual war tactic was used by civil rights activists in the 1950s and '60s. If a person wanted to participate in a sit-in, they went through an extensive non-violence course facilitated by different organizations like SNCC (Student Non-Violent Coordinating Committee), SCLC (Southern Christian Leadership Convention), NAACP (National Association for the Advancement of Colored People), and others. The participants were taught not to retaliate on the basis that the perpetrators would not have anything to fuel their fire. Human behavior dictates that a person can be aggressive longer if the opposing force is aggressive also. On the other hand, if the opposing force isn't fighting back, the perpetrator will tire more rapidly. Use your force field. Resist.

Lastly, when you have to address your situation, choose your words carefully. Remember, it was someone's reckless words that got you into the predicament in the first place. Don't let your reckless words keep you there. Find scriptures dealing with your dilemma, and confess God's promises over life daily. Confess scriptures like Psalms 34:19; Psalms 27:2, 5; Psalms 55:22; Psalms 56:4; Psalms 91:5; Psalms 121:2–8, etc. It doesn't matter how long this unfairness has been rendered. Take God's promises in Joel 2:25 as your own. He will eventually restore unto you the years that the locusts, cankerworm, caterpillar, and the palmerworm have eaten. And some good news: the word *restoration* there does not just mean to get back what was lost, but those things lost plus interest (Exod. 22:4). Be encouraged, you're coming out of this!